Second Sight

Brandon Robshaw

Published in association with
The Basic Skills Agency

Hodder & Stoughton
A MEMBER OF THE HODDER HEADLINE GROUP

Acknowledgements
Cover: Stuart Williams
Illustrations: Jim Eldridge

Orders: please contact Bookpoint Ltd, 39 Milton Park, Abingdon, Oxon OX14
4TD. Telephone: (44) 01235 400414, Fax: (44) 01235 400454. Lines are open
from 9.00–6.00, Monday to Saturday, with a 24 hour message answering service.
Email address: orders@bookpoint.co.uk

British Library Cataloguing in Publication Data
A catalogue record for this title is available from The British Library

ISBN 0 340 74236 4

First published 1999
Impression number   10 9 8 7 6 5 4 3 2 1
Year   2004 2003 2002 2001 2000 1999

Typeset by Fakenham Photosetting Ltd, Fakenham, Norfolk.
Printed in Great Britain for Hodder & Stoughton Educational, a division of
Hodder Headline Plc, 338 Euston Road, London NW1 3BH by Athenaeum Press,
Gateshead, Tyne & Wear.

Contents

1

Bored, Bored, Bored!

Connor was bored.
He was on holiday with his parents.
They were renting a large old house
in a small fishing port.

The fishing port was called Oldshore.
There was nothing to do in Oldshore.
No cinema. No funfair.
No night life. No young people.
Just a few old fishermen.

There was the sea, of course.
But that was usually too rough to swim in.
All you could do was look at it.

There was lots of scenery to look at.
Hills and cliffs and bays.
His parents loved scenery.
But Connor didn't think much of it.
When you'd seen one view,
you'd seen them all!

The house was very old and very big.
All the furniture was dark and old.
The rooms were full of shadows.
In the hall, a large grandfather clock
ticked loudly.

The house stood on the edge of a cliff,
overlooking the sea.
All day and all night,
you could hear the waves
crashing against the cliffs.

And then there was the cry of the gulls.
The wild, sad cry of the gulls.
It gave Connor the creeps.

Two weeks here!
He didn't think he could stand it.
If only something would happen!

And then, one day, something did!

2

Home Alone

It was pouring with rain.
Connor's parents liked going for long walks
along the cliffs,
looking at the sea.
They did it every day.
But even they didn't want to walk in the rain.

'Let's go to the Museum of Country Life,'
said Connor's Mum.
'It's got lots of old farming tools in it.'

'Yes, and it's only an hour's drive away,'
said Connor's Dad.

'You must be joking,' said Connor.
'Drive for an hour
to look at a few old farming tools?
No way!'

'Where do you want to go then?'
asked Connor's Mum.

'I want to go home.'

'Well, you can't,' said Connor's Dad.
'You either come
to the Museum with us,
or stay here on your own.'

'All right,' said Connor.
'I'll stay here on my own.'

He watched his parents drive away,
over the hill, in the pouring rain.

He made himself a sandwich.
He switched on the television.
But there was nothing on.
Nothing he wanted to watch, anyway.

He wandered from room to room.
The house felt very empty and quiet.
All he could hear was the rain
tapping at the windows.
And the clock ticking in the hall.
And the waves against the cliffs.

Then he heard another sound.
It was coming from the room above.

Connor knew he was alone in the house.
But it sounded like footsteps.
Footsteps walking to and fro.

3

Cobwebs and Dust

Connor's heart was beating fast.
He had to find out what was going on.
He had to find out who was upstairs.
Slowly, he climbed the stairs.
His legs were shaking with fear.

To his surprise, he found
the landing covered in dust.
It looked as if no one had been there for years.

There were cobwebs on the walls,
cobwebs hanging from the ceiling.
They hadn't been there that morning.
What was going on?

The footsteps were coming from the door
at the far end of the landing.
Clouds of dust rose up
as Connor walked towards it.

As he got near, the footsteps stopped.
Connor stopped too.
He waited by the door,
wondering if he was brave enough
to push it open.

There was no sound
but the steady ticking of the clock in the hall.
And outside, the muffled roar of the sea.

Connor took a deep breath.
Very slowly, he pushed the door open
and looked into the room.

A man stood at the window
with his back to Connor.
He was looking out at the sea.

There was nothing else in the room.
No chairs. No table.
No bed. No carpet.
Just bare floorboards and dust.

Connor stared at the man's back.

He was a tall, broad-shouldered man.

Connor had a strange feeling

that he had seen him somewhere before.

Connor was scared the man would hear him

and turn round.

He took a step backwards.

A floorboard creaked loudly.

'Who's that?' said the man sharply.

He turned round.

Connor froze in horror.

The man had no eyes.

Just black holes where his eyes should be.

Just empty, staring sockets.

With his arms stretched out in front of him,

the man began to walk towards Connor.

4

Running Scared!

Connor was frozen to the spot.
The man came slowly towards him.
His hands reached out for Connor's face.

Connor screamed.
He turned and ran from the room.
He ran along the dusty landing
and down the stairs.
He opened the front door
and flung himself through it.

The rain was cold upon his face.
He looked up at the window.
The man was standing there again,
gazing out with his blind eyes.

Connor turned and ran down the road.
The rain beat upon his face.
The sound of the sea was in his ears.

Then he heard another sound.
It was the sound of a car coming towards him.
As it drew near,
Connor saw that it was his parents' car.

The car stopped
and Connor's Dad stuck his head out.

'What's the matter?' he asked.
'Why are you running?'

Connor opened the door
and flung himself into the back seat.

'Just drive!' he said. 'Let's get out of here!'

'Where do you want to go?' asked his Dad.

'I don't care!' said Connor.
'Just don't take me back to the house!'

'What's happened?' asked his Mum.
'What's the matter?'

5

Fear of Blindness

That was the end of the holiday.
Connor refused to go back to the house.
His parents tried to reason with him.
They told him he must have imagined it,
or dreamed it.
Connor's Dad went back
and searched the house
and said that there was nobody there,
with eyes or without them.

But Connor could not forget what he had seen.
The man with his black, empty eye sockets
and his arms outstretched,
walking over the dusty floorboards towards him.

The blind man came back to him in nightmares,
for years afterwards.
All through his teenage years,
he would wake up screaming from it.

He had a terrible fear of going blind.
He wore sunglasses all the time,
even in the middle of winter.
People thought he was wearing them
to try and look cool.
But he wasn't.
He was wearing them to protect his eyes.

When Connor left school,
he went into the fire service.
He liked the uniform.
Especially the helmet and mask.
That would protect his eyes all right.

6

Connor at Work

Connor liked being a fireman.
He liked the excitement of it.
When there was a big fire
and the alarm bell went off
and he slid down the pole
and jumped into the fire engine
and they raced down the road
with the siren going,
it was the most exciting job in the world.

Of course, he never went near a fire
without his safety mask on.
Not that there was a big fire very often.
About once a month, if that.
The rest of the time was spent
dealing with cats stuck up trees,
heads stuck in railings,
that sort of thing.

Sometimes he went into schools
to give talks on fire safety.
Connor liked doing that.
He told the kids about the dangers of fire.
He talked about burns,
especially to the face and eyes.

He got on well with the other firemen.
His parents were proud of him.
Yes, it was a good life being a fireman.

Until the accident.

7

Fire! Fire!

The alarm bell went off.
Connor grabbed his jacket
and slid down the pole.
He jumped onto the fire engine.
He put his helmet and safety mask on.
They raced down the road with the siren going.

Connor's heart was beating with excitement.
But he wasn't afraid.
Not with his safety mask on.

'This is a serious one!' shouted the Fire Chief.
'There's a house on fire
with the family trapped inside.
We'll have to go in after them.'

They reached the house.
Smoke and flames
were pouring out of the windows.
They unwound the hose
and aimed it at the flames.

'I'm going in!' said Connor.
'OK – but you'd better not go alone,'
said the Fire Chief. 'Bill will go with you.'

The two firemen kicked the front door down
and went in.
The hall was full of smoke.
They heard screams coming from upstairs.
They ran upstairs and found the family
trapped in a bedroom,
surrounded by flames.

Connor carried the father and daughter out
and Bill carried the mother and son.
'Are you all right?' asked Bill.
'Yes – thank God!' said the woman.

'I'm going back in!' said Connor.
'I saw someone else in there.'
'Wait!' shouted Bill. 'Stop!
There's nobody else in there!'

But it was too late.
Connor had run back into the blazing house.

8

The Accident

Connor ran upstairs,
through the choking smoke.

He made his way to the room
where he had seen a man
standing by the window.
There he was, standing with his back to Connor.

'Come on!' shouted Connor.
'We've got to get out!'

The man turned round.
Connor's blood froze in his veins.
It was the man of his nightmare –
the man with no eyes.
Just black holes where his eyes should be.
Just empty, staring sockets.
He stretched out his arms
and began to walk towards Connor.

Connor screamed.
He turned and ran.
In his panic, he ran the wrong way.
He ran along the landing back into the fire.
Flames leaped around him.

The roof was falling in.
A blazing beam swung down
and smashed into his face.
It shattered his safety mask.

Connor saw a bright orange light
and then blackness.

Then he fell to the floor.
The next thing he knew,
Bill was dragging him down the stairs.
'Keep calm,' said Bill.
'The ambulance is coming.'
Connor blacked out again.

When he woke up he was in hospital.
He tried to open his eyes but nothing happened.
'What's going on?' he asked in alarm.
'Why can't I see anything?'
'You've had an accident,' said a voice.
'I'm afraid you've lost both your eyes.'

9

Back to Oldshore

Connor got a good pension
from the Fire Service.
A very good pension.
It was enough to buy a house with.

His parents wanted him to live with them.
But he wanted to live on his own.
He couldn't be happy,
and there was no point
in making others unhappy.

He decided to go and live by the sea.
He wanted a bit of peace and quiet.
He had had enough excitement.

He went back to Oldshore and
asked about houses in the area.
It turned out that the house
he had stayed in as a boy
was for sale.
Why not? thought Connor.
There was nothing to be afraid of now.
Not now the worst had happened.

He bought it and moved in.
He never went out. What was the point?
He had his groceries delivered once a week,
so he didn't need to go to the shops.
And what was the point in going out for walks,
when you couldn't see the scenery?
He could just as well walk inside the house.
He spent hours
walking to and fro upstairs, thinking.

He never bothered to clean the house.
Dust gathered everywhere
and cobwebs hung from the walls.
But why should he care?
He couldn't see them.

He liked to stand by the upstairs window,
looking out to sea.
He couldn't see anything.
But he could hear the sound of the waves
and the wild, sad cry of the gulls.

One rainy day,
after walking to and fro for a while upstairs,
he went to the window and stood there,
seeing the sea in his mind's eye.
Suddenly, he heard a floorboard creak
behind him.
'Who's that?' he said sharply.

He turned round.
He knew there was someone there.

He walked towards the sound
with his arms outstretched.
He heard a scream,
then the sound of footsteps running away.
The front door slammed.

Strange, thought Connor.
But whoever it was had gone.

He went back to the window
and gazed blindly out at the sea,
listening to the rain.